DESMOND COLE
GHOST PATROL

GHOULS JUST WANT TO HAVE FUN

by **Andres Miedoso**
illustrated by **Victor Rivas**

LITTLE SIMON

New York London Toronto Sydney New Delhi

LITTLE SIMON
An imprint of
Simon & Schuster Children's Publishing Division
1230 Avenue of the Americas, New York, New York 10020
First Little Simon paperback edition March 2020
Copyright © 2020 by Simon & Schuster, Inc.
Also available in a Little Simon hardcover edition.
All rights reserved, including the right of reproduction
in whole or in part in any form.
LITTLE SIMON is a registered trademark of Simon & Schuster, Inc.,
and associated colophon is a trademark of Simon & Schuster, Inc.
For information about special discounts for bulk purchases, please contact
Simon & Schuster Special Sales at 1-866-506-1949 or
business@simonandschuster.com.
The Simon & Schuster Speakers Bureau can bring authors to your
live event. For more information or to book an event contact the
Simon & Schuster Speakers Bureau at 1-866-248-3049
or visit our website at www.simonspeakers.com.
Designed by Steve Scott
Manufactured in the United States of America 0220 MTN
2 4 6 8 10 9 7 5 3 1
This book was cataloged by the Library of Congress.
ISBN 978-1-5344-6109-3 (paperback)
ISBN 978-1-5344-6110-9 (hardcover)
ISBN 978-1-5344-6111-6 (eBook)

CONTENTS

CHAPTER ONE

DANCE, DANCE

"School dance." Talk about two words that should never *ever* be in the same sentence!

Seriously, is there anything worse than a school dance?

Here is how every school dance in the history of dances has ever been.

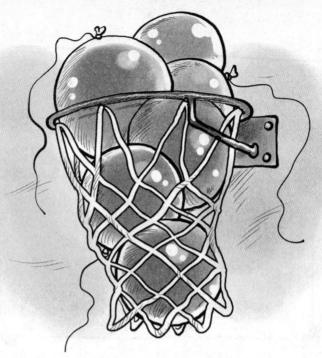

First, they always have the school dance in the gym. The basketball nets are still there, but do you think we're allowed to play basketball? Of course not! All the balls are locked away. Why? Because we're supposed to dance, not have fun!

Second, nobody ever dances. No, that's a lie. There *are* people who dance . . . the grown-ups! It's *so* embarrassing. And they always try to get the students dancing too. No, thanks.

Third, the music is always really old. And really, *really* bad! At every school dance, they have a DJ who plays nothing but songs adults love. The kids have never heard of any of those songs, except when we get stuck listening to our parents' music on long car rides.

It's the worst!

And fourth, we have to dress up. I'm talking suits, ties, jackets, dresses, and shiny shoes that are way too tight and way too slippery, especially on the gym floor.

Plus, gym teachers always get mad because there's some weird rule that you can't wear dress shoes in the gym.

I guess the shoes leave scratches on the *precious* floor. But isn't that what floors are for . . . stepping on?

The whole thing makes no sense!

Don't get me wrong. There *are* some okay things about school dances. There's free food, going to school *at night*, and having fun with your best friend.

ANDRES
MIEDOSO

DESMOND
COLE

Like mine, Desmond Cole.

That's him on the dance floor. My name is Andres Miedoso, and I'm next to him.

The only problem is that we're not just dancing. We're trying to save everyone's lives! Do you want to know what are we saving them from?

It's a long story.

CHAPTER TWO

DISCO DANGER

It all started on a boring day. I was home, looking out the window as the rain ruined a perfectly good bike-riding afternoon. There wasn't anything to do. I couldn't even read because my ghost had stolen all my books.

Yeah, you heard me right. Ghosts are real. A ghost named Zax haunts my house, but not in a scary way. He isn't like that. He's more like an annoying brother.

Another thing I can tell you is that ghosts love to read. But they never return books. I've lost so many books since Zax showed up!

Anyway, since I couldn't go out in the rain and I had zero books to read, I decided to play some video games. I had just started a game when there was a knock on the door.

It was Desmond Cole, standing there soaked from head to toe. That was just from walking from his house to mine, and he lives next door! For him to come over through bad weather like this meant only one thing: Something *huge* was going on.

Desmond came inside, hung up his raincoat, and pulled me into the living room.

"I just found out the school dance theme," he said excitedly.

"What?" I asked.

I was definitely *not* looking forward to the school dance.

But I guess Desmond was, because he raised a hand in the air and kicked one leg to the side.

"Disco Fever!" he said, spinning around.

I couldn't tell if he was dancing or if he had stubbed his toe. Either way, it looked ridiculous!

"I love disco dancing," Desmond said. "My parents play disco music all the time, and they taught me every funky move."

He clicked his heels together and started twirling both of his hands.

My parents played disco music too, but they never taught me how to dance.

"I don't like funky dances," I told Desmond. "Actually, I don't like *any* dances. I like to just find a nice solid wall to lean against and nod my head to the music."

"Do you know *how* to dance?" Desmond asked me.

I shrugged. "Well, um, no."

"That's what I thought," Desmond said. "So I brought my portable speaker with me."

Soon, disco music was blast-
ing through my house. The *thump*,
thump, *thump* of the beat made my
mom's flower vase jump, jump, jump
on the coffee table.

I had to admit, the song was kind
of bouncy. And fun. And I started to
like it.

Even Zax flew into the room. "I love disco!" he screamed over the music.

Desmond pointed at me and yelled back, "Andres doesn't know how to dance."

Zax laughed. "I can teach you!"

And he did! Who would have guessed that ghosts can get funky?

For the next hour Zax showed us all kinds of dances. The music was loud, and we were having so much fun, but then there was another knock at the front door. The funny thing was that it wasn't a normal knock. It was kind of funky too! Whoever was knocking was doing it with lots of rhythm.

Quickly, Zax clicked off the music and shushed us.

"Don't answer that door," he whispered.

It was clear from the look on his face that he was scared. And if a ghost was scared, so was I.

Our boring day wasn't going to stay boring for long.

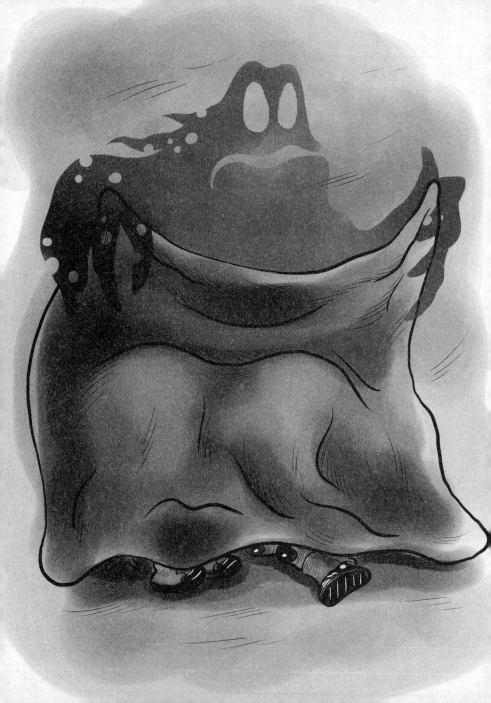

CHAPTER THREE

DEAD BOLT

"Shhh." Zax swooped down low and turned off the lights. Then, before we could ask what was going on, Zax tackled Desmond and me to the ground and covered us with a blanket.

Desmond whispered, "What's going on, Zax?"

"Shhh," Zax hissed again.

A creaking noise came from outside on the front porch. Whoever was at the door wasn't going away.

The knock struck again, but it wasn't a funky knock.

This time it *BOOMED*! I could feel the whole house shake.

That's when I remembered something. "Oh no," I said, and I squirmed out from under the blanket. "The front door is unlocked."

I knew what I had to do. Without thinking, I raced over to the front door and locked the dead bolt. Then I crouched by the door and hoped whoever was out there would go away.

A second later the doorknob started to turn. Someone was trying to open the door! I had no choice. There was only one thing I could do. I screamed for my mom!

I mean, isn't that what any normal kid would have done?

Mom came downstairs with a worried look on her face. "*Mi hijo*, why did the music stop? What is going on?"

When she looked in the living room, I was hiding by the door.

Desmond was under a blanket. Zax had disappeared. She must have thought we had gone crazy. But I needed to warn her.

"Mom," I said, "there's someone outside!"

CLICK.

The dead bolt unlocked, and the door slowly opened. I gasped, until I heard, "Hello, Miedoso house!"

It was the cheerful voice of . . . my dad!

I breathed a huge sigh of relief, and Desmond popped his head out from under the blanket. Something didn't make sense. Could it have been my dad all along?

Or had someone else been out there?

That was when Desmond ran out of the house, still under the blanket. He started looking around outside. I went out there with him, but nobody was there.

I looked up to my window. Zax was
gazing down on us with a ghost face,
which told us what we already knew.
He was totally freaked out, and only
one thing could help him: the Ghost
Patrol.

CHAPTER FOUR

THE BOOGIE MAN

Desmond and I were officially on the case!

Our first stop: Zax. We needed to find out what he knew and why he was so scared.

We ran past my mom and dad, straight upstairs to my bedroom.

Zax was floating and shivering near
the ceiling. And let me tell you that a
shivering ghost is really frightening!

I closed the door, and we waved
Zax down.

"You have to tell us what's going
on," Desmond said.

Zax floated closer and whispered, "It was the Boogie Man."

"The Boogie Man?" Desmond and I repeated.

"Zax," I said, "the Boogie Man isn't real. Back when I was little, I used to think the Boogie Man hid under my bed at night. I made my parents check to make sure he wasn't there. That was the only way I could fall asleep. Now I know he was just make-believe."

Desmond laughed and shook his head. "Um, that's not the Boogie Man. The Boogie Man is some creep who collects kids' boogers!"

"Ew," I said. "That's disgusting!"

"It's disgusting and true," said Desmond. "I saw the booger eater at the park one time. He was leaning against a tree, picking boogers. That was when I started chasing him!"

"You didn't!" I said. But I knew Desmond did. He was always trying to chase down trouble.

"Yes, I did," Desmond said. "I screamed, 'Stop, you booger eater!' but he kept running away. Finally I caught him, but it was just a guy jogging in the park. The Boogie Man is real, though. Now, why would he come to your house? Are your boogers tasty?"

"Yuck, no!" I gave a nervous chuckle. "I mean, I don't know. I don't eat boogers."

That's when Zax put his cold ghost hands on my shoulders.

"There's nothing funny or silly about the Boogie Man," he said gravely. "The Boogie Man doesn't hide under your bed. And he doesn't eat boogers. It's so much worse than that."

Desmond and I stared at him. It was hard to breathe.

"What does he do?" I whispered.

"The Boogie Man . . . ," Zax started, scanning the room to make sure we were still alone. "The Boogie Man dances."

CHAPTER FIVE

TWO GHOUL FEET

HA! HA! HA!

Okay, we lost it. Desmond and I cracked up and couldn't stop laughing. There was nothing scary about dancing. I mean, I couldn't dance, but I was never afraid to do it. I was just afraid that other people would *see* me dancing!

But that's a whole other type of fear!

"This isn't funny! Dancing can be dangerous!" Zax huffed, but that made us laugh even harder.

The ghost rolled his eyes and floated through the ceiling into the attic.

When he was gone, we calmed down.

"Andres, maybe we shouldn't have laughed," Desmond suggested. "Zax was trying to be serious."

"I know," I said. "Let's go get him." We found Zax in the attic next to an old record player. Desmond and I sat next to him.

"Sorry, Zax. That wasn't cool," Desmond apologized.

I nodded. "Yeah, we're ready to listen. Who is the Boogie Man?"

Zax took a deep breath. "This is a true story. It happened a long time ago at the Haunted Ball."

"The Haunted Ball?" Desmond asked.

"It was a big ghost dance at the Kersville graveyard," said Zax. "It was *the* place to be! There was a skeleton band and a foggy dance floor. Every ghost in town came out for it."

I gulped. A ghost dance in a graveyard . . . Sounds perfectly normal for Kersville.

"It was fine at first," Zax said. "Then a stranger strolled in. A very *strange* stranger! He was dressed in a white suit, and he was wearing a thick gold chain with a medallion hanging from it."

I tried to picture this stranger at my front door. It made me shiver.

"And his hair!" Zax continued. "You should have seen it. It was thick and combed into a huge pouf on top. He really stood out in the crowd."

"You're making him sound cool," said Desmond.

Zax nodded. "He *was* cool—*too* cool. He was . . . the Boogie Man."

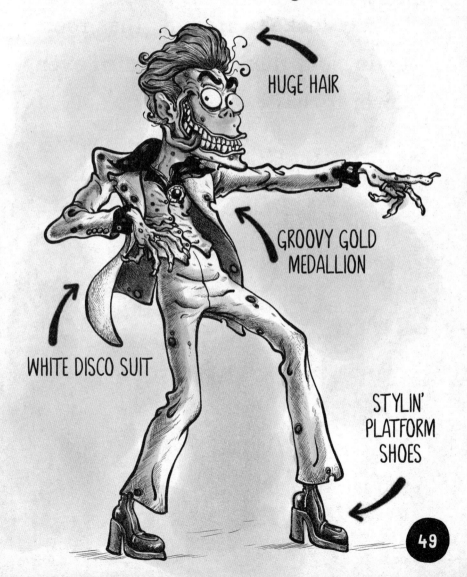

HUGE HAIR

GROOVY GOLD MEDALLION

WHITE DISCO SUIT

STYLIN' PLATFORM SHOES

"So, if he's cool, why would you hide from him?" I asked.

Zax looked around the room again, and then he leaned in even closer to us.

"When the Boogie Man stepped on the dance floor, he started tapping his toes. All the ghosts watched him. It was like we couldn't look away. Then he pointed to the band with a long, thin finger and said, 'Drop the beat.'"

"Then what happened?" I asked. I mean, this story was weird, but not as scary as I thought it was going to be.

"All the ghosts started to dance," said Zax. "Ghosts shimmied and square-danced. They danced the jitterbug and the jive. They even bopped and belly danced!"

"What's so bad about that?" Desmond asked. "It sounds fun."

"What was so bad was they couldn't *stop* dancing," said Zax. "Even the band couldn't stop playing. The Haunted Ball had turned into what is known as . . . the Never-Ending Dance."

Desmond's mouth flew open, but he didn't say anything.

Zax's voice dropped down to barely a whisper.

"Even now, the Boogie Man searches for dances, waiting to strike again."

I threw my arms into the air and asked, "What are we supposed to do about it?"

"There's only one thing you *can* do," Zax said. "You have to stop the school dance. If you don't, every student at Kersville Elementary will be stuck dancing . . . forever!"

CHAPTER SIX

TRAP DANCING

Desmond and I went back to his garage, aka Ghost Patrol Office, the next day. We needed to figure out how to stop the Boogie Man.

Desmond was in his deep-thinking mode. He studied a large map hanging on the wall.

Then he grabbed nets, lamps, and all kinds of gadgets. I didn't know what any of it was for, but I could see that Desmond was making a plan.

I knew what he was trying to do.

"Desmond, are you going to get the school dance canceled?"

"No way," Desmond answered quickly. "I look forward to the school dance every year. And I'm not about to let some dancing ghoul ruin our good time!"

I swallowed hard. Just thinking about the Boogie Man was making my heart break dance!

"Follow me," Desmond said with a smile on his face. "We have work to do."

We walked around to the back of his house.

If you've never seen Desmond's backyard, you don't know what you're missing! He has a full-blown obstacle course back there. It has everything he needs for Ghost Patrol training . . . except for ghosts.

There was a warp wall, a rock wall, and a ropes course, too. The ropes course wasn't my thing. I can't tell you how many times I've gotten stuck up there.

Desmond pulled four full-length mirrors from behind the warp wall and set them into the shape of a box, with the mirrors on the inside.

Don't ask me why Desmond had four full-length mirrors in his backyard. I've learned never to ask questions like that. There was always a reason. Desmond Cole was prepared for anything and everything.

Once the mirrors were set up, Desmond aimed four differently colored lights over the top and turned them on. It looked weird from the outside, but when I stepped into the mirror-box, I could see what Desmond was doing.

It was a miniature dance party in there! Plus, the mirrors made it look like a million of me were waiting to dance.

Next, Desmond pulled out a giant speaker and two pairs of earmuffs. "Put these on," he said, handing me one set. "They will muffle the sound when I turn on the music. Then we'll hide and wait."

I was confused. "Wait for what?"

"The Boogie Man," Desmond said matter-of-factly.

Now my heart was back doing backflips!

Desmond explained, "If the Boogie Man wants to dance, let's bring him here. Then he'll get trapped in our mirror-box! If no one can see him dance, then Kersville will be safe from catching dance fever."

His idea made a lot of sense. I grabbed the earmuffs and followed Desmond to our hiding place, but I still couldn't believe what we were doing. If Desmond's plan worked, the Boogie Man would be here in no time.

And Desmond Cole's plans always worked!

CHAPTER SEVEN

FEEL THE BEAT

We hid out on the ropes course. Desmond said being up that high would let us see when the Boogie Man arrived. Now, I'm scared of heights, but I didn't mind being that far off the ground. Not if it meant I wouldn't be close to the Boogie Man.

When we were settled, Desmond asked, "Are you ready?"

I nodded, and we adjusted our earmuffs. Suddenly, I couldn't hear a thing except for the sound of my own breathing.

That was when Desmond turned on the music and cranked it up all the way. I couldn't hear it, but I could feel the thumping of the bass as it echoed through my body. Even birds and squirrels scampered away!

That music had to be *loud*!

Desmond and I watched the mirror-box and waited. I didn't realize I was holding my breath until my head started getting fuzzy. I had to gasp to get some air.

Desmond put his finger to his lips, motioning for me to keep quiet. Though I had no idea who could hear me over the music.

We turned our attention back to the mirror-box, and good thing we did because right then, we saw something shuffling out from behind the bushes.

It was a ghoul dressed like . . . well,
it was hard to describe. I had never
seen clothes like that! He had on a
suit with crazy shoes that made him
taller than he already was. And his
hair was wavy and wild.

I went to give Desmond a high five. That was when I kind of lost my balance. It was okay though. I was strapped into a safety harness. Desmond always says safety on the ropes course is very important.

But the look on his face was what made me shiver. His eyes were so wide, and he had a big smile on his face. He looked like he was hypnotized by the music!

There was no doubt about it. This ghoul had to be the Boogie Man!

He was dancing up a storm even before he got to the mirror-box. I felt my own feet start to bounce. Luckily, I stopped as soon as he stepped inside.

Desmond and I watched and waited . . . then watched some more. The Boogie Man didn't come out. It was amazing. Desmond Cole's idea totally worked!

Of course, nothing is safe when you're dealing with the Boogie Man. Sure, the harness caught me. Then it swung me right into the mirror-box!

I came in like a wrecking ball, knocking everything over! I broke the mirrors, shattered the lights, and even unplugged the speaker. When the music stopped playing, the Boogie Man stopped dancing.

Me? I hung in the air like an unwound yo-yo.

The Boogie Man walked over to me—closer and closer. Slowly, he reached out, took my earmuffs off, spun me around, and said, "Groovy moves, my man. I dig your swing style."

Then that ghoul did a twirl, snapped his fingers, and pointed at me. "I'll see you at school tomorrow. Save the last dance for me."

Then he boogied away.

CHAPTER EIGHT

HEY, DJ

Sometimes the best plans don't work.

At school the next day, we begged our teachers to call off the dance. But we couldn't exactly tell them why. There was no way they'd believe there was a dangerous, dancing Boogie Man on the loose!

The teachers just laughed us off and said they would see us on the dance floor. It was no use. Grown-ups just don't get this monster stuff.

After school, Desmond walked home with me. "There's no other choice, Andres. If the dance is in danger, then we need to save it."

He was right, but I tried not to
show him how scared I was. The
Ghost Patrol was all that stood
between Kersville and the Never-
Ending Dance.

When we reached our houses, I nodded to Desmond. We needed to get dressed, Ghost Patrol dance-party style.

My parents always made me dress up for dances. I had to wear a tie and a nice button-down shirt.

But I kept on my favorite sweatshirt and jeans. Then my mom combed my hair for a long time. When she was done, it looked a little bit like the Boogie Man's hairstyle!

HUGE HAIR

FANCY-SCHMANCY SHIRT AND TIE

MY BEST RED SWEATSHIRT

STYLIN' SNEAKERS

I bounced over to Desmond's house. He answered the door, and I couldn't believe what he was wearing. He was fancy, but he was also dressed for ghoul-battling action.

READY-FOR-ACTION ATTITUDE

SPIFFY TUXEDO TEE

HIS BEST CARGO PANTS

HIP HIGH-TOPS

At school, Desmond and I headed straight for the gym. Now, the gym at Kersville Elementary wasn't like other gyms. As a matter of fact, our school wasn't like other schools, either.

KERSVILLE

Before it was a school, it was a mansion. The town's founder lived there. After that, it was a hospital.

Now it's a school, but seriously, it's one of the weirdest schools I've ever been to!

The gym was in the mansion's
old barn. And it usually *looks* like a
barn. But not that night! It had been
completely transformed into a disco
on the inside!

I couldn't believe it!

The first thing I noticed was the dance floor. It was a glowing checker-board of lights that flickered in different colors. Above the dance

floor was a disco ball that reflected the light and beamed in every direction. There was even a smoke machine pumping out fog.

"This is going to be the coolest school dance *ever*!" I exclaimed, smiling big as I looked around the gym.

Desmond leaned closer to me and whispered, "Don't forget why we're here: to stop the Boogie Man."

I gulped. Why did he have to remind me?

"Do you have a plan?" I asked.

Desmond laughed. "I *always* have a plan," he said.

Suddenly, a loud voice boomed out of the speakers. "Party people! Are you ready to hip, hop, and groove, Kersville Elementary?"

It was the DJ. All the kids cheered back to her, and the music started.

Bass and drums pumped throughout the gym. The rhythm was catchy. I felt my body start to move to the beat. It was the weirdest thing. I was not the kind of kid who liked to dance.

I panicked. *Oh no! Is the Boogie Man here already? Are we too late?*

Then I looked at Desmond and calmed down. He wasn't dancing at all. I guess it was just the music that was making me want to dance.

And that's just what I did. It didn't even matter that I didn't know how to dance. I was too busy having fun.

Maybe I was having a little *too* much fun. Maybe that's why I didn't see the danger until it was too late.

The Boogie Man was already out on the dance floor, and he was tap-tapping his toes! There was nothing we could do to stop him.

The Kersville Elementary school dance was absolutely, positively, 100 percent *doomed*!

CHAPTER NINE

DANCE OFF

Here's a fact: The Boogie Man has a long tongue. A long *blue* tongue!

As he moved wildly on the dance floor, his tongue hung out like the crazy ghoul he was.

Pretty soon, all the kids were on the dance floor too.

They grooved right next to the Boogie Man. Even Desmond and me!

Here's another fact: Dancing with the Boogie Man is hard. Really *crazy* hard!

Things got out of control so fast. Everyone was moving, and we couldn't stop, no matter how hard we tried. Our bodies had been taken over by the power of the Boogie Man.

Kids were dancing on the tables,
knocking over the trays of cookies
and the huge punch bowl with the
fruit cocktail floating in it.

Even the teachers and parents were dancing, but they had their eyes closed. They didn't even know what was going on!

After a few songs, my feet started hurting. I did one more funky twirl on the dance floor and looked at Desmond. "We're going to need that perfect plan now!" I sang out.

Desmond nodded and did a backflip over to the Boogie Man. He yelled over the music, "Hey, ghoul drool! I challenge you to a dance off!"

Instantly, the music paused, and everyone stopped, except for the grown-ups, who kept dancing and humming to themselves.

The Boogie Man raised his long blue hand in the air. "You look like a groovy opponent. The dance off begins now!"

The beat dropped back in, and I covered my eyes. No one wants to see their best friend get into a dance off with the Boogie Man. But that night I learned something new about Desmond Cole.

That kid could *dance*!

We all watched as Desmond salsa danced, ballroom danced, and Bollywood danced. He danced the Electric Slide, too! You name it—he danced it.

But it still wasn't enough. The Boogie Man was doing everything Desmond was doing. And more!

There was no way Desmond could beat him—not by himself.

So I joined Desmond on the dance floor and boogied too!

The Boogie Man looked surprised.
Then all the rest of the kids joined us.

The next thing we knew, that ghoul
started sweating, then he started to
lose his breath. His dance moves
slowed down until he finally stopped.

The Boogie Man gave up, and everyone cheered!

We'd saved Kersville!

As he walked off the dance floor, the Boogie Man smiled and said, "Thanks for the dance, dudes and dudettes."

CHAPTER TEN

BOOGIE DOWN

Once we showed the Boogie Man that we knew how to move, his dance curse was lifted. Turns out that all he was looking for was a good time with good dance partners. Luckily, Desmond Cole knew how to boogie down!

Actually, the Boogie Man is a cool guy. He comes over to my house for dance parties sometimes. Even Zax gets in on the fun. He's not afraid of the Boogie Man anymore. In fact, they're friends now.

Do you want to know the best thing about the Boogie Man? He loves teaching us new moves. We even learned a few ghost dances.

We learned the Scary Shuffle, the Creepy Krump, even Deep Haunted House Music dancing, and something there wasn't even a name for.

We got pretty good, but there's no way we could do any of these at the next school dance.

The gym teacher would never allow us to dance on the ceiling!